WALT DISNEY PRODUCTIONS
presents

The Emperor's New Clothes

Random House **New York**

Library of Congress Cataloging in Publication Data
Walt Disney Productions presents the Emperor's new clothes. (Disney's wonderful world of reading #29) A retelling of Kejserens nye klaeder, by H. C. Andersen. Two dishonest weavers sell the vain emperor an invisible suit of clothes. [1. Fairy tales] I. Andersen, Hans Christian, 1805-1875. Kejserens nye klaeder. II. Disney (Walt) Productions. III. Title: The emperor's new clothes. PZ8.W186 [E] 74-34485 ISBN 0-394-82568-3 ISBN 0-394-92568-8 (lib. bdg.)

Manufactured in the United States of America

1 2 3 4 5 6 7 8 9 0

BOOK CLUB EDITION   C   D   E   F   G   H   I   J   K
                                        7 8 9
                                        R

Once there was an emperor
who loved to dress up in fine clothes.
He cared more about clothes
than anything else in the world.

The emperor had
a different robe

for every hour
of every day.

These robes filled one whole floor
of his palace.
But still he wanted more.

One day two weavers came to see the emperor.
They said they could weave a very wonderful cloth.
"It is not only beautiful," they said,
"but it is also magic."

"Magic!" cried the emperor.

"Yes," said the weavers. "Only wise men
can see it. Fools cannot."

"Hmmm," thought the emperor.
"If I had a robe made of that cloth,
I could quickly find out
which of my people are fools."

So he told the weavers
to start work at once.

The emperor let the weavers work
on the royal loom.

He gave them the best silk thread
and the best gold thread.

But the weavers
did not use the thread
to weave cloth.

Instead, they put it
into their bags . . .

. . . and the loom stayed empty.

They sat and did nothing,
for they were not weavers at all.
They were planning to trick the emperor.

After a few days, the emperor began to wonder
about the cloth.

So he sent his prime minister to look at it.

The prime minister went into the room
where the weavers were pretending to work.

He looked at the empty loom.

"Dear me!" he thought. "I can't see the cloth!
Does this mean I'm a fool? If so, I must not
let anyone know."

The weavers said to the prime minister,
"See how beautiful this cloth is."
"Oh, yes!" said the prime minister.
"Such fine work! And so many colors!"

But the prime minister
really did not see a thing,
for there was nothing
on the loom to see.

The prime minister went back
to the emperor.

"The cloth is beautiful," he said.
"It is the finest cloth I have ever seen."

The emperor was pleased.

After a few more days, the emperor sent
his general to see the cloth.

The general went into the room
where the weavers were pretending to work.

He looked at the empty loom.
"Dear me!" he thought. "I can't see
the cloth! Does this mean I'm a fool?
If so, I must not let anyone know."

He went back to the emperor and said,
"The cloth is beautiful! It is the finest cloth
I have ever seen."

The emperor was pleased.

"I'll have to see that wonderful cloth
for myself," he said.

The emperor went to the room where the weavers were pretending to work.

He took his prime minister and his general with him.

"Isn't the cloth beautiful?" said the prime minister.

"Look at all those colors!" said the general.
But they were just pretending to see the cloth.

The emperor looked and looked at the loom.
"I can't see the cloth!" he thought.
"Does this mean I'm a fool?
If so, I must not let anyone know."

So he said, "The cloth is more beautiful
than any I have ever seen! You must
make me some clothes at once. I will
wear them in the next parade."

"Very good, Your Royal Highness,"
said one of the weavers. "Let us measure you."

The emperor took off his robe.
The weavers took out
their measuring tapes.

"Thirty-two inches here,"
said one weaver.

"Seventeen inches there,"
said the other weaver.

Then the weavers pretended
to take the cloth
off the loom.

"Your Royal Highness,"
said the first weaver,
"would you like the cloth
to hang this way?"

"Oh, yes," said the emperor.
"That's fine."

"Your Royal Highness,"
said the other,
"do you like the robe this short?"
"No, no" said the emperor.
"Make it a little longer.
Yes! That's perfect!"

The emperor was so pleased that he gave
the weavers twenty bags of gold.

"If I like the finished clothes," he said,

"I will give you twenty more bags of gold."

The weavers smiled.

Now the weavers pretended to work harder than ever.

They stayed up all night cutting and sewing.

Finally they said, "The emperor's new clothes are ready."

On the day of the parade the weavers
came to the emperor's room.
They held out their empty arms.

"Here are your new clothes," they said.
"They are as light as air."
"Beautiful!" cried the emperor.

He gave the weavers twenty more bags
of gold.

Then the emperor
took off his old clothes.
The weavers pretended
to dress him in the new ones.

"Your Royal Highness,"
said one weaver,
"what do you think
of the sleeves?"
"They are wonderful!"
said the emperor.

"Is it too tight
around the waist?"
asked the other weaver.
"Oh, no,"
said the emperor.
"It feels fine!"

He walked back and forth in front of the mirror.
"Yes," he said, "the clothes are a perfect fit!"
But the emperor really had nothing on
except his underwear.

The emperor's men bent down
and pretended to lift his train.
They held their hands high,
carrying a train that was not there.

And so the parade began.

Crowds of people came
to watch the parade.
They all wanted to see
the emperor and his new clothes.

"People say the clothes are magic," said one man.

"People say that fools cannot see the clothes," said a woman.

Everybody was wondering, "Will *I* be able to see them?"

At last the emperor marched out of the palace.

All the people cried, "Oh! How beautiful
the emperor's new clothes are! What pretty
colors! What a perfect fit!"

But of course no one could see any new clothes.

Just then a little girl shouted,
"But he hasn't got any clothes on!"

"Did you hear that?"
someone asked.
"The child says
he has no clothes on!

She's right! The emperor is in his underwear!"

"The emperor has no clothes on!" the people
began to shout.

"He's wearing his underwear!"

The poor emperor heard them.
And suddenly he knew that they were right.

He was the fool!
He had been tricked.

But there was nothing he could do now.
So he kept on marching.

All the time
he was thinking,
"Just wait until
I get my hands
on those weavers!"

But it was too late.

The weavers had already run off
with the forty bags of gold.
They were no fools!